This book belongs to:

....

ISBN 978-1-84135-196-4

Published by Award Publications Limited,
The Old Riding School, The Welbeck Estate,
Worksop, Nottinghamshire, S80 3LR

www.awardpublications.co.uk

10 3

Printed in Malaysia

Award Young Readers

The Three Billy-Goats Gruff

Rewritten by Jackie Andrews
Illustrated by John Bennett

AWARD PUBLICATIONS LIMITED

There were once three billy-goats who lived in the mountains, where wild flowers grew and eagles had their nests. There was Big Billy-Goat Gruff, Little Billy-Goat Gruff and Baby Billy-Goat Gruff.

The three Billy-Goats Gruff roamed the high places each day searching for sweet grass and herbs to eat.

One day, they came to a deep river. They looked across and could see a meadow full of long, juicy grass on the far side.

The grass looked wonderful, and the three billy-goats were very hungry.

"The water looks very deep," said Big Billy-Goat Gruff, "but there is a bridge. We can cross that to get to the other side."

Baby Billy-Goat Gruff wanted to cross first. *Trip trap, trip trap*, went his little hooves on the wooden bridge.

Now under this bridge there lived a very nasty troll. Whenever he heard footsteps on the bridge, he shouted, "Keep away, or I'll gobble you up!"

And so no one had tried to cross the river for years.

But now, here was Baby Billy-Goat Gruff
happily trip-trapping across.

As soon as the troll heard him he bellowed,
"Who's that trying to cross my bridge? Keep away,
or I'll gobble you up!"

Baby Billy-Goat Gruff was very frightened. But he said to the troll, in a very small voice, "Please let me cross the bridge. My brother, Little Billy-Goat Gruff, is coming next. He's much fatter than me."

The greedy troll thought about this. Baby
Billy-Goat Gruff did look rather small. The troll let
Baby Billy-Goat Gruff cross over into the meadow,
and he settled under the bridge again to wait for
Little Billy-Goat Gruff.

The people who lived nearby were amazed to see Baby Billy-Goat Gruff in the meadow. No one had dared to cross the bridge since the troll came to live beneath it. All their children were taught not to try to cross the bridge – not even to fly their kites in the meadow.

"Be careful of the troll," they were told. "Don't cross the bridge – not even to gather flowers in the meadow."

So they were surprised to see Baby Billy-Goat Gruff in the meadow, but they were even more surprised when Little Billy-Goat Gruff came along and began to cross the bridge.

Trip trap, trip trap, went Little Billy-Goat Gruff's hooves on the wooden bridge.

"Who's that trying to cross my bridge?" shouted the nasty troll. "Keep away, or I'll gobble you up!"

He looked so terrible that Little Billy-Goat
Gruff almost turned and ran back.

Instead, he stood bravely on the bridge and
spoke softly to the troll.

"Please don't gobble me up. Big Billy-Goat
Gruff will be along soon. There is much more of
him to eat."

The greedy troll thought about this.
"All right," he said. "I'll wait."

And he allowed Little Billy-Goat
Gruff to cross into the meadow.

He settled under the bridge again to wait for Big Billy-Goat Gruff.

Big Billy-Goat Gruff was now very hungry. He had climbed back up the hill so the troll wouldn't see him watching.

He could see the river from the hillside, and as soon as Baby Billy-Goat Gruff and Little Billy-Goat Gruff were safe in the meadow, he trotted down to the bridge.

Trip trap, trip trap, went his hooves as he ran on to the bridge.

The nasty troll heard him.

"Who's that trying to cross my bridge?" he shouted. "Keep away, or I'll gobble you up!"

Big Billy-Goat Gruff snorted and stamped and bellowed.

"Just try it!" he said, and he lowered his head and – *whump*! – butted the nasty troll right off the bridge.

The troll fell down, down into the river. He disappeared into the water with a great *splash*! and was never seen again.

Baby Billy-Goat Gruff and Little Billy-Goat Gruff
ran to meet Big Billy-Goat Gruff as he trotted over
the bridge into the meadow.

"We knew you would beat the troll," they said.

All the people came out of their houses and
ran into the meadow. They could cross the bridge
as often as they liked now: there was no nasty troll
to stop them.

They brought honey cakes, carrots and little cream cheeses for the three billy-goats to eat, and the children put flower chains round their necks.

The three Billy-Goats Gruff spent the rest of their days in the beautiful meadow and everyone was happy.